Monst Treac

Written by Amy Sparkes

Illustrated by Steve Brown

Collins

It's Mama Monster's birthday
and as she loves to eat,

the monster children want to make

a mega monster treat!

So Monster B checked in her book.
"We need fresh fruit to chop."

"This will do," said Monster Q.

"A brown suit from the shop."

"Throw it in," said Monster B.
"We need some sweet fruit cake."

"Count on me!" called Monster E.

"I've got a garden rake!"

Then Monster B looked in the book.
"We need a bright fresh carrot."

When in the gate came Monster K.
"I've found a preening parrot!"

Monster B sat down to think.

"What could we use for peas?"

Then with a hive came Monster Y.
"I've found some buzzing bees."

"What is next?" asked Monster B.

"Look, we need three eggs."

With sticks and glue came Monster X.
"I've made some wooden pegs."

They smashed and bashed,
and creamed and stirred,
and added runner beans.

"Oh no!" screeched all the monsters.
"Now the feast is turning green!"

Just then the parrot chased the bees
and tipped the pepper in.

Then when the monsters licked the spoon, they threw it in the bin!

The mix tasted just dreadful,
not a mega monster treat!

And so, the monsters all agreed ...

"It's fish and chips to eat!"

21

A monster treat

23

After reading

Letters and Sounds: Phase 5

Word count: 210

Focus phonemes: /ai/ ay, ey, a-e, /u/ o-e, /igh/ i, i-e, /ur/ ir, /oo/ ui, u-e, ew, ue, /ow/ ou, /e/ ea, /o/ a, /oo/ oul, /oa/ ow, /ee/ ea, /ar/ a

Common exception words: to, the, she, we, me, said, so, do, when, what, oh

Curriculum links: PSHE

National Curriculum learning objectives: Spoken language: listen and respond appropriately to adults and their peers; Reading/Word reading: apply phonic knowledge and skills as the route to decode words, read accurately by blending sounds in unfamiliar words containing GPCs that have been taught, read common exception words, read other words of more than one syllable that contain taught GPCs, read aloud accurately books that are consistent with their developing phonic knowledge; Reading/Comprehension: develop pleasure in reading ... making inferences on the basis of what is being said and done

Developing fluency

- Your child may enjoy hearing you read the story. As you read, emphasize the rhythm and rhyme in the story.
- Now ask your child to read some of the story again, reading with appropriate expression.

Phonic practice

- Turn to pages 14–15. Ask them to point out words that contain the /ee/ sound? (*creamed, beans, screeched, feast, green*)
- Talk about the different ways that the /ee/ sound is spelt in these words. (*ee, ea*)
- Now do the same thing with the /ai/ sound on pages 2–3. (*birthday, make*)

Extending vocabulary

- Ask your child to spot the synonyms below. Which is the odd one out?
  - screech   run   scream   (*run*)
  - chased   tipped   poured   (*chased*)
  - threw   chucked   gate   (*gate*)

Comprehension

- Turn to pages 22 and 23 and look at the items that were used to make the monster lunch. Ask your child if they can remember what the items were meant to be and whether they can spot those in the images too.